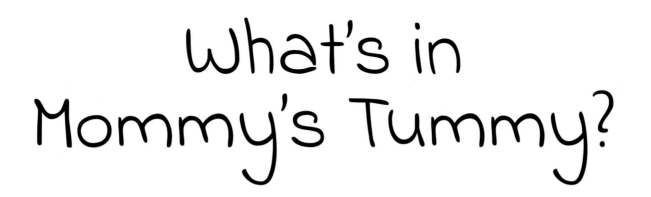

What's in Mommy's Tummy?

Words:
Abby Johnson

Pictures:
Stephanie Alianto

FOCUS
ON THE FAMILY®

A Focus on the Family
resource published by
Tyndale House Publishers

For manufacturing information regarding this product, please call 1-855-277-9400.

For information about special discounts for bulk purchases, please contact Tyndale House Publishers at csresponse@tyndale.com, or call 1-855-277-9400.

ISBN 978-1-64607-156-2

Printed in China

31 30 29 28 27 26 25
7   6   5   4   3   2   1

What's in Mommy's Tummy?

Mommy's tummy seemed to be getting BIGGER and BIGGER, little Luke noticed.

Luke wondered what could be in there.

Whatever it was, if it kept getting even bigger, his mom looked like she might burst!

Luke really wanted to know what was growing in Mommy's belly. He had some ideas.

"Is it a CAT?" he
asked his mom.

His mom giggled.
"No, it's not a cat."

"Is it a DRAGON?"
Luke asked.

His mommy
laughed.

"No, it's not
a dragon."

Luke tried to guess again.
Maybe if he thought hard
enough, he could somehow
make his dream come true.

"I know what it is," Luke exclaimed.
"It's a BaBY KanGaRoo!"

His mom clutched her growing belly and laughed
so loud that it surprised little Luke.

"It's definitely not a kangaroo," she said.

Luke was becoming
frustrated.

First he wanted a CAT
to add to their family.

Then he wanted a DRAGON. That would be so cool. And a BABY KANGAROO would have been even better!

But none of those things were growing in his mommy's belly.

Luke started to worry. He had heard of bad things that grow in people's tummies that can make them sick.

"Is it something bad, Mommy?"
Luke asked.

"Like when someone has to see a doctor?"

Luke remembered when his grandpa caught a flu bug and had to go to the hospital. He didn't want his mom to catch any BUGS or GERMS—or something that his mom called a virus. Now he was really concerned.

Luke's mom told him not to worry.

"Germs and viruses can live inside a person's body," she said, "and some can even eat the things you are eating and make you very sick."

"Like all the pizza and ice cream you have been eating?" Luke asked.

"Sort of," Mommy said with a laugh. "But don't worry, it's not germs growing in my belly."

Now Luke was
really confused.

If his mom wasn't sick, and it wasn't GERMS or a DRAGON or a KANGAROO or a CAT growing in her tummy, then what was it?

Luke's mother sat next to him on the couch. She looked into his eyes and explained what was happening.

"Luke, the only possible thing that could be growing in my belly is a baby brother or sister for you. Isn't that exciting?"

Luke thought for a moment.
A BABY brother or sister would be very cute.
But as cute as a KANGAROO?

He wasn't sure. But he started to get excited
as he thought about playing with a new BABY.

(And good thing it wasn't a virus, because that would be no fun!)

But Luke was still thinking about that dragon. "What if I keep wishing for a DRAGON?" Luke asked. "Will the BABY in your belly become a DRAGON?"

"Nope," said Mom.

"But what if I say it's a DRAGON over and over again? Will it be a DRAGON then?" Luke asked again.

"Still no," Mommy said with a laugh. "Human mommies can only have human babies. Just like cats can only have kittens and dogs can only have puppies. Can you imagine if a dog had a human baby?"

Luke started laughing at the thought. How silly that would be!

Luke felt a little silly for even thinking those other things were growing in his mommy's belly.

But his mom assured him it was okay to ask all those questions because, after all, he was just a little boy who wanted to know the truth.

Luke had just one more
question to ask his mom.

"I'd like to grow a BABY
in my belly, too," he said.
"Why can't boys have babies?"

His mom smiled and said, "God designed it so that only mommies can have babies growing in their bellies.

But guys like you and Daddy get to protect mommies and help them with their babies, which is a very important job."

His questions answered,
Luke cuddled up to his
mommy and her growing
belly. He whispered,
"I can't wait to meet
you, little BABY."

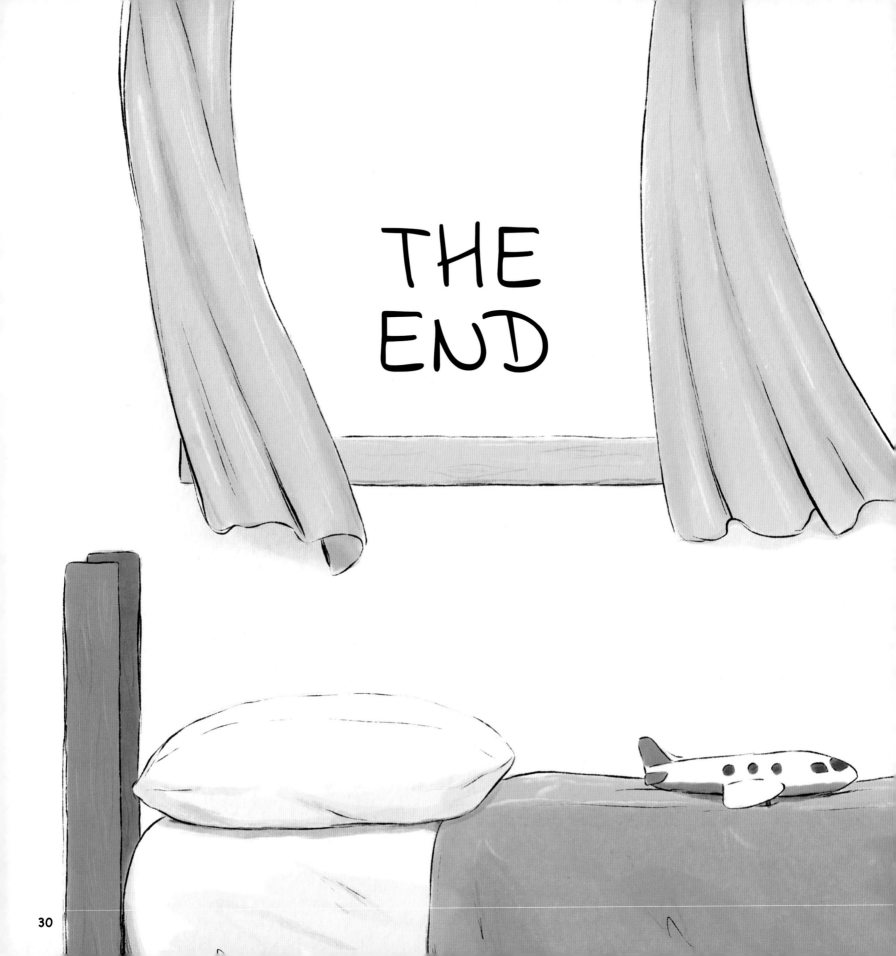

Discussion Questions

1. Why can't the mommy have a KANGAROO or DRAGON in her tummy?

   Repeat the question with younger children to ensure they understood the message.

2. Who makes BABIES?

   God created babies, and they have value because He made them. It doesn't matter whether they are a boy or girl, light skinned or dark skinned, abled or differently abled, etc.

3. Genesis 1:24 tells us that God made it so only humans have human BABIES and only animals have animal BABIES. Why do you think that is?

   God is a good God and knew that human mommies and daddies would know best how to care for human babies.

4. How can we celebrate BABIES?

   We can pray for mommies and babies yet to be born, throw a baby shower for pregnant mommies, bring baby supplies to a church nursery, etc.

5. Did you know we can see BABIES while tucked away in the mommy's tummy?

   Share an ultrasound picture of your child, or do an online search for images of a baby's developmental stages.

Parenting is a journey that starts before you even meet your baby—and it never ends. If you're looking for more resources to help you navigate the many stages of parenthood, **look no further . . .**

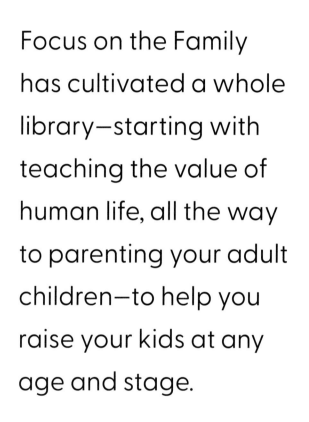

Focus on the Family has cultivated a whole library—starting with teaching the value of human life, all the way to parenting your adult children—to help you raise your kids at any age and stage.

Scan this code to access our **free** parenting resources.